# REAL STORIES OF A SOLDIER

## AS ARUNACHALAM

notionpress
.com

INDIA • SINGAPORE • MALAYSIA

ISBN  979-8-88606-897-9

# Contents

# I

# A SALUTE TO THE MOTHER ELEPHANT

Most of our Indians know about the place "Kanyakumari", where the Arabian Sea, Bay of Bengal and the great Indian Ocean meet. The world-famous Indian Philosopher, Swami Vivekananda, got his "Mukti" at this place of confluence of the three Seas. The sunrise and sunset on these Seas is a panoramic view, and it is worth watching. The ancient and very famous historical temple "Devi Kanya Kumari" also adds another feather to the cap of Kanyakumari Town. Every day, there are large crowds of tourists, not only from India but also from the world, visiting Kanyakumari. I am always proud to say that I was born and brought up in a village near Kanyakumari.

My ambition to join the army also came true in November 1971. The Indo-Pakistan war had started at that time, and there was a call from our Nation to youngsters to join the Army. I took that opportunity to join the Army and got selected. The Military training at a Military Training Centre was very tough, and from there, I was posted to Arunachal Pradesh after completing my training. "What a coincidence? My name is Arunachalam, and I was posted to a place in Arunachal Pradesh?" I thought. My friends congratulated me and said, "Arunachal, you are a fortunate person to get your posting to your home station of Arunachal Pradesh." "No, my friends, it is only a coincidence in name; otherwise, my native place is very far away from Arunachal Pradesh, and it will take six days to reach my place from Arunachal Pradesh," I explained.

After a long and continuous train journey for three days, I reached the nearest railway station in Arunachal Pradesh, Tinsukia(Assam). My place of work was Lohitpur, which was very far away from Tinsukia. My travel to Lohitpur was fascinating. I boarded the army bus, and the journey was so pleasant.

The army bus passed through a huge tea garden, and it was spread through a vast area, say, 10 kilometres from one end to another. For me, it looked like the enormous ground area was covered with green carpet. Hundreds of ladies were very busy plucking tea leaves. They wore a huge traditional cap which was made of bamboo strings. These standard caps protected them from rain. They carried funnel-type gigantic baskets on their backs also made of bamboo trees, as bamboo was very common in this area. I saw a giant King Cobra crossing the road at one place, and the army bus stopped until King Cobra crossed the road. I was terribly shocked to watch King Cobra and worried about the fate of people who were working as labourers in the vast tea garden.

It was a rainy season, and I had to cross seven rivulets to reach Lohitpur. The Army vehicle dropped me at the bank of one river, which spread over a distance of one kilometre in width. The current of the river was swift, and the waves were massive, and that was the first time in my life I had seen such a large river.

"Where did the river flow from? I enquired a Boatman, who was busy preparing the boat for our sailing to the other side of the river. "What are you going to do if you know about that?. He did not care for me. But I learned that the river flowed from the great Himalayas; some parts of the mountain were covered with snow. Anyway, the expert Boatman safely navigated the big boat, and we reached the other bank of the river. I again boarded another Army vehicle waiting for us, and it moved slowly and cautiously as the road was muddy. The army vehicle crossed a village, and we reached another bank of the river we had to traverse. While crossing the village, I saw a lush, green forest. The banana plant was easily twelve feet or more, and its huge wide leaves were around nine feet long and two feet wide, and there were bunches of yellow fruit. Due to frequent rain in this area, the forest was full of bushes and shrubberies. It was dark even in the daytime because the foliage of trees was very close to each other and formed a thick canopy that even sunlight could not pass through.

Elephants moved in large numbers, and gigantic as they were, they always ground food very easily in the forest. Here, Elephants were brought up like domestic animals. Whenever people wanted to go to another place, they caught hold of the elephant in the forest, which they trained as their pet animals, and the whole family rode on the large mammal to travel from one place to another. A boat is not required to cross small rivers, but elephants are used to make one's way across such rivers. There is no need to feed the elephant as it will venture into the forest for food and eat until it is satisfied.

Another forest animal in this area is a python. Many times, it visits the village by mistake. But, the villagers never harm either the python or the elephant, and they do not harm the villagers. Finally, after crossing so many hurdles, like, carrying our personal luggage on our heads and crossing the river by walking into the knee level water of another river, I reached my place of work.

"Welcome to Lohit," my colleague said. I breathed a long sigh of relief and exchanged our pleasantries. "How are you living without electricity?" I said. He cautioned me, "Here, life is not easy. It rains very often, and frequent flooding in the nearby river is very common. You should be very careful with wild animals like tigers, elephants and pythons. Remember, you are not an ordinary citizen; you are a soldier and have come here to defend our country against enemies. Do not expect comfort for your life," said my senior. They strictly told me to restrict my movement during the night as wild tuskers roam our area. "Oh my God, I was thrown from heaven to hell," I said to myself. Anyway, as a combatant soldier, I was ready to accept whatever came my way. The place was freezing, and during winter, one cannot sleep or rest without warm clothing.

One day, I got up at midnight to attend my natural call. It was completely dark, and one could not see what was on his way. As I wandered through the darkness, I dashed against a gigantic rough and tough object. My mind worked very hard and fast to know the rough and tough object and realised that it was an elephant standing without any movement or sound. I immediately rushed back. "Oh Lord Ganesha, save me," murmuring these words, I went back.

When I told my friends about the incident, they took it very casually and said, "Such incidents are widespread here. The elephants will not harm you unless you harm them. But, small insects, like worms, are very dangerous. They are leeches that look like a small thread and stick to your body and suck your blood very slowly without your notice. You will come to know the sucking of your blood when its thread size becomes like a rope of one-inch diameter and one feet length. So, be careful of small insects," he said.

My life in the thick forest of Arunachal Pradesh went on quite normal for some days. Then, one day, my friend Balu came to me and broke out news of terror and said, "Arunachal, one mighty mother elephant has become mad and is on a foray. It is harming the people who come her way. Be careful." I took his advice with a pinch of salt, but I never thought I would be a close victim of the same elephant on the foray.

I wanted to find out the reason for the mother elephant's aggressiveness. It destroyed huts, harmed people and randomly attacked all places. People panicked, and one village man in that area told me about the whole incident of the mother elephant's aggressiveness. The flood in the nearby river village was not seasonal, as the flood might come without any reason, like heavy rain or melting of ice from the nearby mountain. The flood might come suddenly and wipe out everything in a short time. In such a situation, one baby elephant, which was with her mother near the river, was swept away. Since the flood came from the upper hill, it was muddy with the high speed of current waves. The baby elephant cried for help from her mother. The efforts of the mother elephant were all in vain as the flood was sudden and unexpected. She had run along the riverside some distance to save her baby but lost her. The flood took the elephant very fast; it was lost from her sight. So, the mother elephant was very sad and became angry. She went on a foray in search of her baby, but she could not find it. After two days, the elephant grew mad and furious. The trumpet of the fierce elephant was horrible, and it started attacking people who came in her way, destroying huts, gardens, and many other things. So, losing her baby is the reason for the mother elephant's madness and all further destruction.

The baby elephant, which was taken away by the sudden flood, was found by the soldiers one kilometer from crossing the river. The soldiers took the baby elephant to their main office, which was very near my accommodation. I went and saw the baby elephant. "Oh! It is tiny, cute, and looks like a large pig," I said. The small head, trunk, legs, and tail resembled Lord Ganapathy. It was lying in a pathetic condition at the corner of a small barrack. Sometimes, it got up and ran in the small barrack from one corner to another like a mad man. The sight of the baby elephant was heartbreaking as it was searching for her mother. There was grass, bananas and sugarcanes around the small barracks, but it didn't eat. It even refused fresh milk, which was offered by the soldiers. The condition of the baby elephant was pitiable as it was alone and separated from her mother. So, it was handed over to the Forest officials for their care and further action. "The mother elephant will come to your place in search of her baby very shortly. Be careful," the forest officials warned us and went with the baby elephant.

The next day, the enraged mother elephant came to our place searching for her baby. It was understood that the baby elephant was kept in the barracks from the food left over by the baby elephant, but its baby was not there. So, the mother elephant destroyed the whole barracks and went away.

"Our aim was to save the baby elephant and unite the mother with the baby. But it was very expensive. The whole base was demolished," said our senior army officer with regret. After searching for its baby, the powerful mother elephant ventured into the nearest forest. The whole episode was conveyed to every soldier in that area through the army channel. "The mother elephant is very dangerous to all of us. It will attack and even kill whoever comes her way. It will not stop her furious activities until it gets her baby. Be careful," they warned us strictly.

One Sunday morning, News broke out from our area that the mother elephant was again seen forayed our area and threatened the lives site there. However, the elephant was driven out of place by our soldiers before my arrival. "The mother elephant is gigantic; muscles are bulging out from her heavy body. Her trunk is very long. It can easily catch people who come her way." commented one of the soldiers. His comments triggered my eagerness to see the elephant by all means. So, my friend Bala, who knew Sanskrit Vedic Shlokas, and I plucked enough courage to go inside the forest.

"Om Shri Ganabathy Bhagwan Jai Ho!, Om! Shri son of Shivji Jai Ho! Om! Shri Beloved son of Ma Parvathi Jai Ho! We both praised Lord Ganapathy in our hearts and ambled into the forest. The forest was very thick as the trees were large in number and were chained to each other. Only a few rays of sunlight passed through the gap in the branches of the trees. Wild grass was seen everywhere, and many thick bushes grew hip-level.

"Bala, our wish to see the mother elephant may cause danger to our lives. If a python is hiding in one of the bushes, it may not be visible to us. But it could take our lives," I said to my friend Bala, and he nodded his head in acknowledgement. After trekking for more than an hour in the woods, we chanced upon the elephant devouring the leaves of a giant banana tree, "What a Godly appearance of the mother elephant, it appears for us that Lord Ganapathy is in front of us." We thought our suffering to see the magnificent elephant had not gone wasted. Our heart was filled with the unknown happiness that we were in heaven. While my friend, Bala, utterly rhymed his Sanskirti song on Lord Ganapathy with his folded hands, I also joined. As we slowly opened our eyes, we could see that the elephant was blessing us by raising her trunk in an 'S' shape. We both were overwhelmed as if we were blessed by Lord Ganapathy. Our joys knew no bounds.

Suddenly, our joy and blessings of Lord Ganapathy went wrong. Due to overjoy, my friend Bala became playful; forgetting his present situation, he took a small broken stone and childishly threw it at the elephant. I never thought, even in my wildest dream, that my friend, Bala, would indulge in such type of mindless act, and then it all happened in the twinkling of an eye.

"What did you do, Bala? Are you mad" I cried in panic. The mother elephant trumpeted and took a sudden turn towards us and started chasing us menacingly, stretching her trunk at full length to catch hold of me and kill me. "Oh! My God, save me, save me," these words came from the bottom of my heart. My loud cry echoed in the silent forest, but there was nobody in the forest except the two of us. There was only a pinhead gap between me and the elephant's fully stretched trunk. I took the advantage and ran like a mad man. The sharp wild grass tore my clothes, and blood oozed out of my body. I did not stop running.

The furious mother elephant was still chasing us. We ran helter-skelter through the dense forest like devoted athletes. My heartbeat rhythm was like the sound of a speeding train crossing the bridge, and my face was damp in sweat due to the fear of death. It was a freak accident, so to say. But the elephant, though, in a frenzy, could hardly keep track of us as the forest was dark and gloomy. The massive elephant could scarcely cross the thick forest and lost track of us. We were saved.

We panted and gasped for breath; we stood speechless facing each other. Few minutes later, I asked my friend, "Bala, what made you throw a stone at our Godly elephant, which we believed to be Lord Ganesha? We were blessed by him, but you have reacted like an evil ghost. Tell me, what happened to you within a second." He was silent for a while and said, "I never realized the gravity of my puerile throw. Within a second, my mind went wrong, and I childishly threw a stone on the elephant as boys threw stones on dogs". My friend did it for fun, but it backfired. Lord Yema, who keeps the accounts of our survival in the world (according to Hindu belief), smiled on us. "Let it remain a nightmarish anecdote," I said.

Now, we were trapped in the sizeable shrubby track of the thick forest; we virtually lost our directions. Due to rain in all seasons, we could see big trees, green grass, and other plants everywhere. The insects were small in size, but their sound was unbearable. Though it was daytime, the forest was dark as the sunlight was blocked by big trees.

"Bala! Large and powerful pythons are very common in this forest. Be careful," I warned. My friend from Arunachal Pradesh told me that one python in the forest swallowed a baby horse even after the mother horse lashed the python several times by its back legs. Like this, several scary stories started pouring into my mind, and I was full of fear. In this situation, my friend Bala went one step ahead of me. He was literally crying with fear.

An eerie silence droned on and on. Now, we didn't know in which direction we were walking. We were surrounded by trees and darkness. We walked zig-zag quite a long distance with prayer on our quivering lips. "Om Shri Ganapathy Baghwan, Almighty God, forgive us. Save us from the forest, take us to our residence". We prayed from our heart and soul. We realised that survival in the world was not in our hands, but God alone could save us. We took a vow that we would not harm anybody. We knew that nobody would come to our rescue in the thickest forest except God alone. So, again and again, we prayed to the Almighty for our safe return.

After a long distance of zig-zag walking, I could see smoke billowing out from one place. I shouted in joy and jumped. The strained pain, fear, and mental worries vanished. "Are you mad?" my friend Bala questioned. "When we are facing death in the forest, you are jumping joyfully," he shouted at me. He thought that I had become mad as there was no way of escape. "Bala, Lord Ganapathy saved us. Our prayers were heard by the Almighty," I said. "Tell me how?" He eagerly wanted to know. "Can you see the smoke billowing out on the right side?" I pointed out to the cloud of black-grey smoke. He acknowledged. "So, what?" he questioned. That is the place of our residence," I said firmly. Bala lost his hope of reaching our site as he worried about the stone he threw childishly at the elephant. He later believed that his stone throw was not on an elephant but on Lord Ganapathy, and he deserved the confinement in the forest.

He asked me in confusion, "How can you say that the smoke coming from the area is our residence?"

"The smoke is from our cookhouse, where preparation for food for all the soldiers is in full swing," I assured him. Bala was overwhelmed. "Are you sure that we will reach our place?" He asked me with great eagerness. "Of course, nobody uses cooking coal except the Army in this area," I said. With great enthusiasm, we ran a distance towards the area and safely reached our place. "Courtesy Lord Ganapathy."

After this incident, days went very peacefully. My friend Bala and I had forgotten the eventful day slowly. After that, our life became normal as we were busy with our day-to-day work.

The furious mother Elephant was in pain as thorns of wild plants were sticking at the four feet. Minor injuries were caused by small trees while the angry Mother Elephant was running through the thick forest. It also pained the elephant as it was exhausted and could not walk. Finally, step by step, slowly, it reached the outskirt of a small village in Arunachal Pradesh and laid down for rest.

The small village was charming at the height of Himalaya Mountain. The people living there were called Mishimi. It is situated 800 metres above sea level. The people of the village are lovely and very small in population. The village was surrounded by forests, and Mithun(Wild Ox) lived in large numbers. They are powerful, and the Mithun is celebrated as a great wealth like Gold. If anybody has more Mithun means, he is a rich man. With this cattle species, old men can exchange two or three Mithuns for beautiful young girls by offering them to their fathers. Drinking of locally made liquor by the people is prevalent in the village.

One young Missimi boy was in love with a missimi girl from the same village. They often met at the outskirt of the village. One day, when the young lovers were at the outskirt of the village, they saw the tired and thoroughly exhausted mother elephant. The lovers immediately went to the spot and helped the wild elephant by removing the thorns from the feet and applying the medicine made out of plants. They made the mother Elephant more comfortable, and the mother elephant came to normal life. The mother elephant blessed the lovers by touching their heads with her trunk. The Mother Elephant was wandering in that area, and the lovers offered fruits and vegetables to the mother elephant, and they got a blessing.

One day news spread in the village that the girl's father had sold his daughter to an old man in exchange for three Mithuns(wild oxen), and the arrangement was being made for the girl's marriage with that man. In addition, the elderly gentleman was `already married. The girl was kept at home, and she was not allowed to go outside. So, she could not meet her lover and the elephant. Her lover could not fight with the villagers. The only way to marry her was to bring four Mithuns(wild oxen), which was impossible for him.

He went to the place where he used to meet his lover and the elephant. He was despondent, and he could not express his sorrow to the Elephant except by crying loudly. Though the elephant has five senses, it realizes that the girl has some problems. The elephant was already in a sombre atmosphere, as it could not meet the lovers for two days, and now the boy was alone and weeping bitterly.

The mother Elephant picked the boy up and placed him on his back and went to the place guided by the lover boy. When it reached the girl's house, it trumpeted. On hearing it, the girl came out of her house. The elephant picked her up, placed her on her back, and walked toward the forest.

The elderly Bridegroom was trying to attack the Elephant with a spear. But the Elephant caught him and threw him in the air. The throw was so severe that the man was hanging upside down on the branch of a tree. The villagers followed the mother Elephant, but after seeing her attack the Bridegroom, they went back.

After venturing into the forest for a distance, the mother Elephant stopped. The lovers got down and prayed for the blessing of mother Elephant, and they were blessed by the lifting of her trunk. Going back to the village would be hell for the lovers, so they decided to go to another village where they were safe.

They comforted the mother Elephant by touching her and feeding her with green leaves and fruits available in the forest. The lovers did not know that Elephant was searching for her baby.

After some time, the mother Elephant started moving to the nearest forest. The lovers also sat on her back and moved with her. Realising the situation, the mother Elephant moved along the edge of the forest to another village for the sake of the lovers. After a few hours, the Elephant trumpeted loudly as it sensed that her baby Elephant was close to her.

"Marvellous!" The baby Elephant was sheltered in the forest office. On hearing her mother's call, the baby Elephant also sounded in a higher tone. The mother Elephant became jubilant and ran very fast to meet her baby. It was so exciting. The baby Elephant was also excited and ran like a mad animal to meet her mother. They united, and there are no words to describe how both the mother and baby were in the highest level of happiness. Forest officers also felt very happy that both mother and baby were united.

The story ends with great satisfaction for everyone as the Baby Elephant was united with her mother, and the lovers were also saved from the villagers.

**The moral of the story**

COURAGE AND PERSEVERANCE CONQUER ALL BEFORE THEM

# II

# A TALK WITH A GHOST

Human beings will generally reach their heavenly abode on attaining old age. This is natural death set by the Almighty. However, early death occurs in some cases due to accidents either by train, road transport, or aircraft. In many cases, mass death is also happening due to war and natural calamities like tsunamis, sudden floods, fire, cyclones, etc. In all the above cases, many people die at a young age. What will be the fate of the souls of people who die earlier than the natural death of old age?

It is the general belief that the soul will haunt the world until the natural death of old age. They are called Ghosts. So, what will the Ghost be doing? The Ghost will very comfortably enter into the body of selected human beings with whom the soul has more attachment and affection and sometimes exhibits its existence. The Ghost may do good things and do harm to others also. In villages, the man believed to be living with a ghost is respected by villagers as the man attached to God.

Has anyone seen a Ghost doing duty in the Army of any Country? Yes, it happens only in India. In the Indian Army, the Ghost of "Baba Harbhajan Singh", who died during the 1962 Indo-China War, still does his duty on Nathula Pass in Eastern Sikkim. In the military camp at Nathula Pass, a camp bed is kept for him, his boots are polished, and his uniform is kept ready every night. It is a great wonder that bedsheets are reportedly crumpled every morning, and boots are muddy by evening. So, it is believed that Baba's Ghost is doing his duty daily.

Even today, jawans posted at Nathu-La post firmly believe that Singh's ghost protects them. Soldiers even believe that his ghost warns them of any impending attack at least three days in advance. Even the Chinese, during flag meets, set a chair aside to honour Harbhajan Singh. Stories about his ghost visiting the camps at night and even waking up the soldiers who sleep while on a watch are massively popular and very regular.

Anyway, it is a matter of people's beliefs. I believe that Ghosts coexist in the world and live with human beings, though one cannot see ghosts. During my Army service, I happened to serve in the border area of our country and experienced the existence of Ghosts.

Thirty years ago, while I was serving in the Chamb Jaurion sector of Jammu and Kashmir State, I moved for War practice in that sector along with my soldiers. During the 1971 Indo-Pakistan War, many soldiers were killed in the Champ Jaurion Sector, and the area for War practice is very close to that Sector. It was 6 PM in the evening, and many vehicles with a massive load of office equipment and personnel luggage were moved towards the training area. All vehicles moved one by one without using the headlights of the vehicle for security reasons. The road was very rough, and hence the movement of vehicles was very slow. So, we could reach our training area at midnight, in other words, zero hundred hours. The area was completely dark, and one could not identify each other but by their voice. Since it was midnight and so all were very tired due to 6 hours long continuous journey on a rough road, we decided to sleep in the open. We started unloading our personal luggage from our vehicles. Two uniform persons appeared before me and started shouting, "This area is ours. We will not allow you to stay here. Move from our area." Their tone was thunderous. I counter-attacked with my high tone and warned them. On hearing my high, loud voice, they became very serious. Though I could not see their faces, their very rough breathing indicated that they were very furious. "NO. It is our land, and we will not allow you to stay here. Move from our area."

I imagined the two were soldiers and would behave inhumanly. I decided not to talk further with these at midnight. So, we moved from the place and slept in a nearby area where they did not object. When all our men were asleep, I could not sleep as my mind was recollecting the argument with the two persons. After a short sleepless night, I had a dream in which two persons with burning torches were jumping high and shouting aggressively. After the dream, I fell into deep sleep due to tiredness.

The following day, when the sun's rays struck my face, I woke up. It was 7 AM. After prayer, I watched the surrounding area. I was greatly astonished to see the site claimed by the two persons was a GRAVEYARD (Burial Ground). So, I realised that the two persons were not human beings but GHOSTS. Since we tried to occupy their graveyard, the ghosts sent us out. The two spirits celebrated their victory with burning torches in their hands. So, ghosts still exist in the world, I believe. There are so many stories still screening in cinema theatres about ghosts. A large number of books also published stories on ghosts. Many people vow that they have experienced ghosts in the world. So the belief in the existence of ghosts depends on one's own mind.

# III

# A SALUTE TO THE HEROES OF OUR MOTHERLAND

I was in Srinagar, Jammu and Kashmir state of India, for two years. "WOW, what a beautiful place!" I said admiringly. Surrounded by mountain peaks, lush green valleys, glistering lakes, temples, and spectacular Mogul–era gardens, Srinagar has inspired many tourists worldwide.

Dal lake of Srinagar is freezing and the best place to see snow, whereas, in summer, it becomes picturesque when flowers blossom everywhere in the valley, snow melts, and trees get into new shapes. The rooftops of the houses are turned into flower gardens. One of the best parts of the Srinagar trip is the houseboat stay. Throughout the houseboat, it is wall to wall Kashmiri carpets used. Tiles are used in toilets. You will find wood carvings in doors, windows and carvings also. Antique decorating lights are provided throughout. You can stay on Houseboats and enjoy the Shikara Ride in the evening. Another place worth seeing at Srinagar is Hazaratpal, where a hair strand of Prophet Mohammed is preserved.

An important place to see at Srinagar is Shankaracharya Temple. It is also known as Jyeshteshwara Temple. It is situated on top of Shankaracharya Hill in the Zabarwan range of Srinagar. It is dedicated to Lord Shiva. The temple is at the height of 1000 feet above the valley floor and overlooks the city of Srinagar.

Though I have many sweet memories of my life at Srinagar, one shocking memory always remains in my heart forever. The very particular memory is related to the sacrifice of a young captain, my neighbour at Srinagar.

During my tenure at Srinagar, life was difficult as "PROXY WAR" by our neighbouring country, and we were always kept on "OP ALERT", wearing combat uniforms and being armed at all times. In such difficult conditions, a young, newly married couple became my neighbour at the Officers' accommodation. The officer was a Captain from an Infantry Battalion. He was very active and fearless and wanted to do heroic action against terrorists. He was least worried about his newly married life and always thought about action against the terrorists. His wife was a post-graduate student from a well-known university looking very simple. She was a strict follower of Hindu Mythology, worshipping God, performing Puja and doing Arthi all the time. She generally avoided lunch and dinner as she used to follow "Fasting" (without food) in the name of God. I understood that all her prayers were aimed at the "Safety" of her husband, who was searching for militants and fighting with them.

The officer served at SOPORE, which was infested by terrorists and away from Srinagar. So, his visit to Srinagar was sudden and unknown to his wife as the officer was on very active service. I helped the young couple by providing my residential telephone to his wife. During that time, the phone was the only service for direct communication as the mobile phone was not introduced. So, it was a great help for the young couple. Moreover, I used to provide a vehicle in case of need to the family as I felt that it was my moral responsibility and duty to help them when the young officer was committed to operational duties for the sake of our Motherland.

Life was normal for some months. Then, one night, when I was returning from my office, I happened to notice a big gathering of officers with their wives near my room. The Captain's wife was crying bitterly in high pitch, and the wives of senior officers consoling her helplessly. She was uncontrollable and inconsolable, blaming the Almighty for not helping her. I immediately understood that her husband would have been killed by terrorists. My eyes welled up in tears and rolled down with great emotion. "Uncle, I have brought fresh apples with leaves, especially for you". His words were ringing in my ears. Both the young officer and his wife would always call me uncle. His body was taken to his home with full honour by Army.

After a few days, I got a letter from the wife of the young martyr. It was a very sorrowful letter demanding justice from God because of having good faith in "HIM" by performing all types of worship and "Fasting". She had written in that letter that she would join Army to take revenge on the killers of her beloved husband. I was confused about whether she would be able to join the Army when she was not recovered from her high grief. So, I replied to her letter with some words of solace and asked her to be cheerful. I also enclosed three First Day covers with folders on the "Param Vir Chakra" series.

My mind always thought of her words, "I will join the Army to take revenge on behalf of her dead husband". Yes, there are ample chances because she is from the place of Jhansi. City, Southwestern Uttar Pradesh state, where Lakshmi Bai, Queen of Jhansi state and a leader of the Indian Military of 1857-1858, fought the British Army. The 22 years old queen Lakshmi Bai Jhansi Rani refused to allow the British to annex Jhansi City.

The British Army surrounded the fort of Jhansi, and a fierce battle raged. She offered stiff resistance to the invading forces. Lakshmi Bai did not surrender even after her troops were overwhelmed and defeated. Lakshmi Bai managed to escape from the fort and headed eastward, where other rebels joined her. Dressed as a man, she fought a fierce battle with British Forces, and she was killed in combat.

So, I was sure that Ladies from Jhansi city would always be daring and successful women. Now, I was fully confident that the wife of the young martyr would definitely join the Indian Army and fight with the enemies like Lakshmi Bai of Jhansi city.

A few years have gone by, and I was also posted to Bhopal as Officer Commanding of a Unit. Again, I got a letter from the young Officer's wife requesting me to attend the Passing out Parade. She had completed her Army training at Officers Training Academy in Chennai. Her parents were already at OTA, Chennai, for the Passing out Parade Ceremony. I greatly wondered about her determination, daring and challenging action. I thought that taking revenge on the killers of her husband may be in her words alone, but not in action. But she proved herself that "she was the real hero of our Army when her husband had already established that "Hero of our Nation". Now, the young woman officer is serving in the "Army Education Corps" as a Major in our Indian Army. Though her services are not directly related to confrontation with terrorists, I am sure it will certainly be a helping hand to those troops fighting against terrorists forever.

# IV
# ENCOUNTER WITH DEATH

It is a ritual for me to take my family for a picnic to a prominent place during my annual leave. So, last year, we visited a crocodile park near Golden Beach in Chennai.

The Chennai Crocodile Park is located 40 km south of the city of Chennai, in the State of Tamil Nādu, India. It was established to save three Indian endangered species of Crocodiles: the marsh or Mugger Crocodile, the Saltwater Crocodile and the Gharial.

This Crocodile Park is the biggest Crocodile sanctuary in India. The Park has one of the world's largest collections of crocodiles and alligators and has bred five thousand crocodiles and alligators representing 14 of 23 existing species, including the three Crocodile species all considered native to India.

The Crocodile Park has 2483 animals, including 14 species of Crocodiles, 10 species of turtles, 3 species of Snakes and 1species of Lizard. When we went to the park, it was feeding time for the crocodiles. When the park helper threw pieces of meat in the bay, the two started fighting with each other to share the meat. It was a very horrible scene where both crocodiles had started piercing and cutting each other with their row of very sharp teeth. At last, the fighting was over when one of them died. My daughter almost fainted on seeing this. After reaching home, when I told of my real encounter with the crocodile in the Eastern part of our country, it took more time for me to bring her back to normal as she was terribly shocked at hearing my real escape from a crocodile.

It happened when I was posted from the Western part of our country to the Eastern corner. After four days of tiresome journey, I reached the transit camp on the outskirts of Silchar, which I had to pass through. Since the season was hot summer, I badly wanted to take a deep dip in water to waive off my train fatigue and the scorching heat. With the direction of a local man, I searched and found a huge isolated pond just a kilometre away from the transit camp.

It was strange that none of the locals was near the big pond; even the cattle were not seen nearby. For a few minutes, my mind was searching for a good reason and then I thought it could be the wrong time as it was mid-noon.

Since I knew swimming, I stripped and dived into the water. I went to a distance of 20 to 30 meters inside the water, and I was shocked that I could not measure the depth of the water even when I had gone to a depth of approximately 15 meters. Now, panic gripped me, and I came to the surface.

By then, a middle-aged woman was shouting very loudly in her local language, stretching both hands towards me. She continued her shouting and started beating her head with both hands. Though I could not understand her language, I sensed some danger and immediately wanted to get out of the pond. Yes, there was considerable danger to my life, no doubt.

I saw a huge crocodile moving towards me very fast from a distance of 30 meters by opening its big mouth, showing all its row of sharp teeth in anticipation. It appeared that the water was giving way to the very silent killer, as its movement was swift like a bullet. With utter dismay, I turned towards the bank of the pond with redoubled efforts and without breath and swam like a mad man. I did not take a chance to look back and lose precious time. Finally, I reached the bank and ran like a world-class athlete to a distance of 100 feet. When I turned around, the crocodile was on the brink of the water. The mouth of the angry crocodile was still open, and the eyes were moving fast to locate its slipped prey.

Hurrah! I escaped from danger, thanked God, and searched for the lady who saved me. I could not locate her. I believed the lady was none other than the Goddess KAALI MAA.

When I started my journey from the Western part of my country to the Eastern region by train, I halted at Kolkata to visit Kolkata Kali Temple to pray for a safe journey to the Eastern corner of my country and also healthy life at my workplace. So, I went to Kali Temple and sincerely believed that Goddess Kali Maa saved me from the crocodile Kolkata Kali Maa.

It is a Hindu temple in Kalighat, Kolkata, West Bengal, India, dedicated to Kali. It is one of the 51 Shakti Peethas where the various parts of Dakshayani or Sati's body are said to have fallen in the course of God Shiva's RUDRATANDAVA. Kalight represents the site where the toes of the right foot of Dakshayani or Sati fell.

On remembering the lady, I thank the Almighty for the providential escape.

# V

# MY JOURNEY IN NORTH EAST

Travel gives a character of experience to our knowledge, and the experience is unforgettable forever in my case. The Naga Tribals are very hard-working, and they follow their ancient tradition in music, dance and costume until today. So, whenever I went through the map of India, I always wanted to know about the remote areas of North East of our Country. My desire was fulfilled when I got a posting to one of the places in Nagaland State. On May 7, 1999, I started my journey from Chennai by train and reached Guwahati, and from Guwahati, I got to Dimapur by road. My trip to Dimapur was delightful when the bus passed through the thick green forest and tea garden. The tea garden is spread over large areas like an ocean. I saw hundreds of women with big round caps made of bamboo splints on their heads and long baskets on their backs working in the garden

Nagaland was inaugurated as the fifteenth state of the Indian Union on December 1, 1963. Almost all the Nagas are Christians.

**DIMAPUR:** Dimapur is the gateway of Nagaland as this is the only Railway Station in the State. One can reach Dimapur by air also from Kolkata. Though it is in Nagaland, people from Assam and Bihar also live at Dimapur. A maximum number of shops close at 6 PM. The movement of people after 6 PM is very thin. During the daytime also, Central Reserve Police Force personnel patrol the area.

There is a big market where electronics, textiles and fancy items made in China are readily available. In New Market, frogs, snakes, oysters, and fish are sold. Each and every street has a church. On Sundays, very smartly dressed parents with children go to church early morning, and the church is crowded. All Naga teenagers look very stylish, wearing western outfits of the latest fashion.

**KOHIMA**.: From Dimapur, I travelled by bus to Kohima, the capital of Nagaland, which is 78 km away from Dimapur. My journey from Dimapur to Kohima was enjoyable as the road leading to the hills is full of trees on both sides. The road was very steep and narrow in some places, with many curves made by cutting the hill. The bus had to cross so many pads of the hill to reach Kohima. The road is constructed and maintained by the Border Road Organization of Project of Sewak. While travelling to Kohima, I saw the river "Dhansari" and waterfalls big and small which adorned the serpentine roads. On reaching Kohima, I felt that Kohima hill station looks like heaven. Here, Naga girls wear western-style costumes, and they look beautiful. They speak English soft with a musical tone. Being the capital of Nagaland State, the road is busy with motor cars and Naga people. The dominating features of Kohima are the War Cemetery, the Cathedral and the Nagaland State museum.

When I was at Kohima, the capital of Nagaland State, I visited the War Cemetery of World War II. I was thrilled to see Kohima's very beautiful and well-maintained war Cemetery. I am sure that there is no such War Cemetery similar to that of Kohima in any part of our country. The War Cemetery is being maintained by the Commonwealth Grave Commission.

The War Cemetery commemorating the death of soldiers in the battle of Kohima is situated on the site of the old Deputy Commissioner's bungalow on the hill. Four terraced platforms have been constructed on which hundreds of bronze plates in size of 15"x10" are fixed in neat rows. During the Burma Campaign in April 1944, the might of the advancing Japanese have finally halted, literally at the door of the Deputy Commissioner's bungalow on the garrison hill, Kohima.

A vast white cross with an inverted sword dominates the Cemetery. The Cemetery ground is a tourist delight where the lawns are tastefully manicured with beautiful flower beds displaying many colours.

The war Cemetery has been constructed in memory of English, Canadian, Australian, Indian and African Soldiers belonging to different Regiments and Corps. On each grave is an epitaph on which the name and details of the glorious deed are hitched. In addition, thoughts and affectionate quotations are also etched on the plaque. Some of the quotes which I remember read as follows:-

"In the morning and at the going down of the Sun, I shall always remember him."

"Deep in my heart, his memory is kept; I loved him too dearly to ever forget."

"Sleep on, beloved; your memory in our hearts still lived."

"At the going down of the Sun in the evening, we will remember him."

"Till we meet again."

"Gone from us but not forgotten, never shall this memory fade."

"He gave his greatest gift, his unfinished life."

"Gone but not forgotten, missed most by those who loved him most."

"He lived beneath these foreign skies, but in our hearts, he never dies."

"Duty done, now at rest."

"Peace, Perfect Peace."

"To the cause of freedom, you gave your all."

"For honours, liberty and truth, he sacrificed his glorious youth."

'He died that you must live."

"It is sad but true; we wonder why the best are always first to die."

The most wonderful writing which has touched a chord in my heart reads:

'WHEN YOU GO HOME, TELL THEM OF US AND SAY, 'FOR YOUR

TOMORROW, WE GAVE OUR TODAY.'

The War Memorial reminds us of the silent warriors who selflessly sacrificed their lives for our tomorrow. In Kohima, around the tennis court of the Deputy Commissioner lies men who fought in the battle of Kohima. They and their Comrades finally halted the invasion of India by the forces of Japan in April 1944.

The memorial at Kohima, constructed half a century ago, is unparallel in design and thought. My mind often questions why we can't have such war memorials for our Jawans who sacrificed their lives for our Motherland.

# VI
# ROLE OF NAGAS IN WORLD WAR II

In February 1944, a Japanese 31st Division invaded Kohima by road. Its Vanguard was approaching Dimapur to cut the lifeline of British forces in Imphal. Hence, the Second Division of the British Army was called from Southern India.

By land, sea, and air, the Division moved to Dimapur. As soon as the troops arrived, they advanced to the relief of valiant Kohima Garrison, isolated on top of Garrison Hill. On April 14, leading the advance of the five Infantry Brigade, smashed the Foremost Japanese roadblock at Zubia. On April 18, six Inf Bde (Infantry Brigade) relieved the Kohima garrison almost at the limit of its endurance.

The first task had been completed. The second and heaviest task was to drive the enemy from the dominating heights of Kohima. On these surrounding hills, war was fought for one month. In the bloodiest and most desperate campaigns here and on the hills above, 6 Inf Bde endured and fought back till every Japanese soldier was killed or lay buried.

To the North, the Kohima village was carried by the night assault of 5 Inf Bde and held against repeated counter-attacks to the south over the steep jungles covering the hills. 4 Inf Bde marched for 14 days to strike the enemy in the heart of its position. By May 15, all of Kohima was liberated, and the strength of the 31st Japanese Division was broken. The victory could not have been won without continuous help from Naga stretcher-bearers, porters, and guides.

There remained the final task of the 2nd Division to complete the rout of the 31st Japanese Division and open the road to the besieged Garrison at Imphal at ARADURA, Kauazma and Thakan. Victories were quickly won against desperate enemy rear guards. On June 22, 1944, contact was made at mile108 with the forces advancing from Imphal. The road was opened, and the 3 months siege of Imphal was lifted. The proud 31st Japanese Division, a routed force, was in a headlong retreat eastwards, littering the road to Japan with its dead and dying.

There around the tennis court of the Deputy Commissioner of Kohima, lie men who fought in the battle of Kohima. They and their comrades halted the invasion of India by the forces of Japan in April 1944.

**THE CATHOLIC CATHEDRAL**: The Catholic Cathedral is situated on top of the hill of Kohima, spreading over 9.13 acres. It is believed that it is the biggest hill station church in Asia. The surrounding area is well maintained with grasslands and flower plants and is very clean. All visitors have photo sessions in this area. A very beautiful stage has been constructed in the centre. There is a huge holy cross of Jesus Christ.

The construction of the church commenced in Feb 1986 and was completed in April 1992. It is situated at 6800 ft above sea level. The total cost of construction was 3 Cores. Sitting capacity is 3000 while standing capacity is 15000. It is massive and looks very natural and realistic. At the foot of Jesus, there is a horn of Mithun (wild ox), showing Naga Culture. On both sides, there are two Naga Spears in a crossed position. We can see a bird view of Kohima City from the church. The aerial view of the church looks like a star. In front of the church, there is an extensive grassland. Below the grassland, there are many stone pillars exhibiting Jesus' life and quotes from the Bible.

**NAGALAND STATE MUSEUM**: Nagaland State Museum is very informative about the Naga Tribes and their culture. They have models of Naga Men and women (life-size) made of wood well displayed. The museum also exhibits different types of tribal dresses, ornaments, some made of ivory, musical instruments made of bamboo splints and metals, various types of weapons used for hunting, and life-size models of animals like tigers, lions, and monkeys, kangaroos, elephants etc. There are numerous tribes among Nagas themselves. Each tribe has its own types of dance and social customs. Even the designs of the Naga shawl differ from one tribe to another. The walls and floors of the museum are made of wooden planks. The walls of some halls are entirely made of bamboo and arranged very beautifully. Naga wooden dish utensils and a few types of Naga smoking pipes, different kinds of headgears made from fine bamboo splints are also displayed.

**PHEK:** From Kohima, I went to Phek by road. It is the district headquarters of Phek District and is located at 5700 ft above sea level. We have to cross many pads of hills, several times up and down the slope. We have to drive the vehicle very cautiously. Travelling from Kohima to Phek is breathtaking as the road is steep and narrow, having so many turns and full of trees and bushes on both sides of the road. In some places, bamboo groves abound. On my way, I saw Naga ladies with their babies on their backs climbing the hills searching for their good earnings. They are hard workers, climbing up and down the hill many times. I also came across young Naga men going hunting with their guns. Every Naga is having the traditional Naga Dah. I saw waterfalls and small rivulets, which make beautiful scenery on the hill. We happened to see a huge black snake crossing the road. One Naga saw the snake and killed it instantly by smashing its head with a big stone. He then put the snake in his bag and walked away. As there is no plain area, these people do ladder-type cultivation on the hills. They get water for irrigation from waterfalls and small reservoirs. In the daytime, insects in the forest make wild sounds, resembling thriller movies. I observed that most of the villages are located on top of the hills. The soil of the hill is very loose, which results in landslides on monsoon days

**IMPHAL**: I left for Imphal from Kohima by road. The road, which travelled from Kohima to Imphal, is a historical monument as Japanese Forces after Imphal reached Kohima by this road. Unlike Phek, the road is straight in most places except for some curves. While travelling to Imphal, I came across many small rivers. Hence, cultivation in this area is on a large scale. While passing through the road, I saw a military convoy of 25 to 30 vehicles with Jawans in full uniform, wearing bulletproof jackets, and carrying arms and ammunitions. The traffic on the road is very heavy as this is one of the main roads from Dimapur to Imphal. Hence, trucks carrying essential commodities are being brought to Imphal by this road.

**GOVINDJI TEMPLE**: The Shai Shai Govindji temple is famous in Imphal town. All VIPs visit this temple frequently. This temple is very ancient. Every day, six times pooja is performed. There are two gigantic bells kept on both sides of the temple. Gillett and Johnston in London made the bells in 1936. The bells ring during pooja time, and the sound can be heard up to 3 miles radius. When I wanted to know about the temple's history, I was told that during the regime of King Bhigalchandra Singh, his uncle, who was much against him, wanted to become king in his place by driving out the Maharaja. He took the help of the soldiers and tried to kill him. The king escaped and reached Agartala and got the asylum of King of Agartala. The uncle ruling Imphal came to know about this and sent a message to the King of Agartala that the man given asylum by him was not the true King but an imposter. So, the King of Agartala consulted the Ministers, and it was decided by the king's court that a mad elephant should test him. The elephant was kept in a large cage. The deposed King was given a fixed date to prove his identity. The King prayed to Lord Krishna day and night. One day Lord Krishna appeared before him and promised to rescue him. The maharaja vowed to build a temple at Imphal for Lord Krishna.

The testing day came, and the Maharaja was sent inside the cage. On seeing him, the elephant came running towards him, making a big sound. There was a big crowd watching this incident who believed that he would be killed by the mad elephant, but to the surprise of all, the elephant bowed its head, sat before him and lifted its leg. The Maharaja climbed on the elephant and moved around the cage. In this way, the king proved his identity. Then, the King of Agartala sent his troops along with the king and made him King of Imphal. As per the promise, the King made this Govindji Temple.

**IMPHAL BUDDI MARKET:** Another important characteristic feature of Imphal is the Buddi Market, where all shopkeepers are old ladies. The ladies are large in number, and they keep goods of all varieties, from textiles to vegetables. This market is very busy with people bargaining with these old ladies. Ladies are active and do good business to support their families. The old women wear the traditional dress of Manipur and gold ornaments like chains and bangle. Some of them have flowers around their foreheads.

**NUPEELAL MEMORIAL** In the heart of Imphal city, there is a memorial called "Nupilal", which pays homage to women patriots involved in the Freedom struggle. There is an enormous statue of women struggling against the British Raj, with an artificial fountain and grassland. It reminds us of the spirit of patriotism of the women of Imphal during Independence.

**CONCLUSION:**Nowadays, the people of Nagaland have evolved according to modern days. Jeans and frocks replace the traditional skirts and shawls. The folk songs are replaced by Western music. They now dance to the tune of pop, rock and jazz music of western countries. People no longer can be seen with feathers or spears in towns. Nagas living in urban areas do not use earthen pots or beautifully carved bamboo caps, but they have shifted to bone china and ceramic items. They are now fast developing due to education. Children go to school and do higher studies. Education has great demand. The hard-working and industrious nature of Nagas cannot be denied. They cultivate high above the mountains, which is not an easy task. Their work starts as early as 5 AM, both in urban and rural areas. But despite all this, the Naga people living deep inside the jungle are traditional and have not forgotten their culture. They still dance to their folk tunes to welcome the rain. These people in the forest have not changed their old traditions and culture, and they are proud of these.

Anyway, my great ambition to see the North East States satisfied lots of pleasure and sweet memories. I enjoyed my journey through the North East States.

# VII

# A GEM IN THE JEWEL

Mukukchung, Tuemsang, Zunebutto, Naginimora, Phek, Wokha, Dimapur and Kohima are the district headquarters of Nagaland State. Though their culture and language differ from one district to another, they are united and cooperative. When I was serving at Nagaland, I visited all these district headquarters and had memorable experiences with the Naga people and their traditional culture.

**Mukukchung:**

It is one of Nagaland's most developed and socially and politically sound cities. Mostly known for its totally extravagant Christmas and New year celebrations, the MOATSU festival is celebrated at the beginning of May. Mukukchung is home to the AO tribe native to the land. The museum in the Arts and the cultural complex is the perfect place to explore the tribe traditions in Nagaland, especially their rich war battle gear and clothing. The city should definitely be on your list of must-visit places in

Nagaland because of the exceptionally highly hospitable tribes and the cultural heritage and folklore that have been maintained throughout the years.

**Tuemsang:**

Located in the eastern part of Nagaland, Tuemsang is a district bounded by five Districts. The Tuemsang town serves as a nerve centre of the Eastern part of Nagaland state. The Town was founded in 1947 to administrate the erstwhile North Eastern Frontier Agency(NEFA) that comprised the present day Tuemsang, Mon, Longleng, Kiphire and Noklak districts. These four districts combined are also known as "Eastern Nagaland". Tuemsang is famous for its rich tribal culture and Warm and friendly people. It is also very well known for its handicrafts and handlooms.

I was travelling in a Nagaland State Transport Bus, which starts from Kohima to Wokha. The road between Kohima to Wokha is very narrow and rough. Since Wokha is on the top of a hill, the bus has to cross so many curves and move the upward direction of the hill. The bus driver was an expert in hill area driving, and I enjoyed the scenery of the hill when the bus was moving in the direction upward. After travelling 10 km, the bus driver stopped at a convenient place. I was in a confusion that the bus was stopped without any reason. After a silence of five minutes, one old passenger on the bus stood up and started praying to Lord Jesus, quoting some phrases from the Holy Bible. The old man prayed for the good health of all the people in the world and requested Lord Jesus for a safe journey. All the passengers on the bus joined in the prayer. At the end of the prayer, all said, "Amen" Then the bus journey continued further. I was very much impressed with the prayer of all passengers for a safe journey and peace in the whole world. Such a type of prayer is generally not being done in other states of our country. Their thoughts are selfless. I believe that they will still continue this traditional habit today also.

During raining season, landslides in the hilly area of Nagaland are common. There was continuous rain in Mukukchang and Tuemsang area for four days, and the road was blocked due to a landslide. Four days Mails for (Mukukchang, Tuemsang and Zunebutto) were dumped at Jorhat Railway Mail Service Office, and the outgoing mails were held up for four days. In those days, mobile service was not available. The only communication available was the BSNL landline. That too was not working due to heavy rain. So, we could not find out the mail position, and we were afraid that there were chances of missing mails at Jorhat Railway Station as mails for Nagaland post offices are dumped in one place due to less space at Jorhat Railway Mail Service. In such a situation, one officer will be detailed to ensure the smooth moving of mails for the hilly areas of Nagaland. So, I was delegated to collect the mails from Jorhat railway station and delivery the mails to post offices of Nagaland hill places.

I went to Jorhat railway station in a Jeep and segregated all mails from the heap of mails. I took the mails of Mukukchung, Tuemsang and Zunebutto and started my journey to Mukukchung. Though we reached Mukukchung safely, we faced a significant roadblock problem between Mukukchung and Tuemsang. Hundreds of small and big vehicles were waiting for the clearance of the roadblock. I went to the roadblock area and saw that a landslide had blocked the road, and the blocked road was so slushy that no vehicle could cross the road. The land slide was so heavy that it would take two days to clear the roadblock, even by mechanism and men. Now, I was worried and could not make any decision, "What to do?" Finally, I decided to cross the slushy mud area with the help of the Naga people.

I surveyed the area and found that a group of young Nagas were singing and dancing in one place. I went to that place and requested the Naga team leader to help us drive the jeep from the mud and slushy area to the other side of the road. I told the leader that the mails were meant for the people constructing roads and maintaining the road in their area. The mailbag was carrying letters from their home, and it will boost their mind and body and certainly create good energy for their task of road clearance.

My words motivated the group leader, and he shouted in his local language and called all the young Nagas who were gathered there. He spoke to them in high spirit. The much-motivated young Nagas stepped into the slushy roadblock and pushed the jeep out from the blocked road with much difficulty and hard work. The jeep was driven out from the roadblock with all mails safely. I breathed a great sigh of relief. But for the young Nagas, their pant and shirt even face was sprayed with mud and slush. They looked like people who had taken a bath in soil and slush water. They were not worried about the damage to their shirts, pants, and even their healthy bodies. They shouted with joy and danced as if they got victory in their task. The team leader came to me and said, "Are you happy?" There were no words to convey my gratitude to the team leader.

Good people are everywhere. The leader of the Naga team looked like a "Gem in the Jewel" to me.

# VIII
## SAVIOUR OF KASHMIR

Brigadier Rajender Singh was born on June 14, 1899, in Bhagoona Village Samba District in Jammu Division. He was an officer in the Jammu and Kashmir State Forces who attained martyrdom on October 26, 1947 fighting during the Indo- Pakistani war of 1947-1948.

He was commissioned into the J&K State Forces as a Second Lieutenant on June 14, 1921. On September 25, 1947, he took charge as chief of Army Staff of J&K State Forces from Major General HL Scott. Brigadier Rajender Singh and his men successfully delayed the forward movement of a much larger contingent of Pakistani regulars and tribal raiders towards Srinagar until the Indian Army arrived.

On December 30, 1949, he received independent India's second-highest military decoration.

# IX

# INVASION OF KASHMIR BY PAKISTAN

After our country's independence, more than 560 small and big Kingdoms merged with India, except for Jammu and Kashmir, ruled by Maharaja Hari Singh. Since Jammu and Kashmir became independent after August 15, 1947, Maharaja Hari Singh removed Major General HI Scott, a British Officer, from the post of Chief of Staff and appointed Brigadier Rajinder Singh, son of the soil, on September 24 1947. It was when the state was in a deep military and political crisis. Hence, Maharaja could not decide to join any one of the dominions, either India or Pakistan. Pakistan already decided to annex Jammu and Kashmir with it. Pakistan took the political and military crisis of the kingdom to their advantage and sneeringly began to prepare a military assault to occupy the Kashmir valley by force.

Pakistan, with a strong force of 6000 troops and tribals, entered the valley in the Muzaffarabad, Uri sector on the night of October 21 and 22, 1947. Two Muslim companies of 4 J & K Infantry of the Maharaja's Army were deployed at the border area of Muzaffarabad for defence. These two Muslim companies of 4 J & K Infantry joined with the invaders instead of fighting against Pakistan. Hence, Muzaffarabad quickly fell without a fight which was a severe blow to the defence capability of Maharaja Hari Singh, and that was a victory for Pakistan.

(Contd.....2)

When Maharaja Hari Singh was informed about the fall of Muzaffarabad, he decided to carry out accession parleys with India for getting reinforcement from the Indian Army. Brigadier Rajinder Singh, Chief of Staff of the Kingdom, volunteered to go to the war front on October 22, 1947. He collected whatever troops were available in Srinagar cantonment and marched towards Uri with a small force of 100 army men. They reached Uri at midnight on October 22 and 23, with much difficulty as heavy rain in the Uri sector. The next day, on October 23, 1947, the first assault on the Pakistani invaders was made by Brig Rajinder Singh with his 100 gallant Jawans at Garhi and inflicted heavy casualties on the enemy but lost a complete platoon in the battle. On October 24, 1947, the most important "Uri Bridge" was blown up by Brigadier Rajinder Singh and his men. The destruction of the Uri Bridge was a significant setback to the Pakistan Army, which blocked their invasion. This destruction hampered the enemy's march as the only route was vehicular based, and hence the operation was delayed. The invaders, however, followed up on foot, and Brigadier Rajinder Singh commenced a befitting attack on them. After delaying the enemy at Mahura on October 25, he took up a defensive position at Rampur - Buniyar, where he gave a determined fight and inflicted significant casualties on them until 0100 hours on October 27, 1947. Since this small force came under very heavy pressure, it was forced to withdraw due to mounting casualties. Brigadier Rajinder Singh himself was hit on his right arm and legs in the ambush while withdrawing to the next position. Despite his bleeding wounds, he inspired his men to fight on.

He was thus able to delay the enemy for the crucial four days, which enabled Maharaja Hari Singh to complete the accession proceedings with India and arrange reinforcement (Army) from India, which actually arrived a few hours after his death. The quick arrival of the Indian Armed Forces at the war front stopped the invasion of Kashmir by Pakistan.

Brigadier Rajinder Singh was the first Chief of Staff to fight with the enemies on War Front till death to save Kashmir from Pakistan, for which he is remembered as the "Saviour of Kashmir". He was awarded the second gallantry award of Independent India, "Mahavir Chakra", posthumously for his courage, supreme sacrifice and leadership.

JAI HIND

# Say 'No' To Drug

Drug Makes Men as Devils
    Mind as Mad
    Health as weak
    Heaven as Hell
    Students as Cannibals
    Rich as Poor
    Then, Why Drugs?
    So, Say "No" to Drugs
    Enjoy life and smile.
    Oh! Drug addict, listen,
    Family call you as dead
    Community mark you as Criminal
    Country treats you as Refugee
    So, Say "No" to Drugs
    Enjoy life and Smile
    Oh, dear students,
    See the beauty of flowers
    How Rose and Lilly
    Flourishes and looks?
    Enjoying the music of
    Bees and Colors of butterfly
    Are they taking drugs?
    So, Say "No" to Drugs
    Enjoy life and smile.
    Oh! Dear people! Say "No" to Drugs
    Bring love and light to the family
    Live like Birds and flowers
    Smile like Rose, dance like Peacock
    Have strength like Elephant
    Bring glory to the Country

So, Say "No" to Drugs
Enjoy life and smile.

● 48 ●